NALL

THE EUREKA MOMENT!

Scientist profile

Name: Marie Curie
(born Maria Salomea Sklodowska)

Date of birth: 7th November, 1867

Date of death: 4th July, 1934

Education: The Sorbonne

Major achievements:

- Discovering the phenomenon of radioactivity
- Discovering the radioactive elements radium and polonium
- Winning two Nobel prizes (in physics and chemistry)
- Becoming the first woman to teach at the Sorbonne
- Pioneering the use of mobile x-rays to examine wounded soldiers on the battlefield

SCIENCE STORIES

Published in Great Britain in MMXIX by
Book House, an imprint of
The Salariya Book Company Ltd
25 Marlborough Place, Brighton BN1 1UB
www.salariya.com

ISBN: 978-1-912537-42-6

© The Salariya Book Company Ltd MMXIX
All rights reserved. No part of this publication may be reproduced, stored in or
introduced into a retrieval system or transmitted in any form, or by any means
(electronic, mechanical, photocopying, recording or otherwise) without the written
permission of the publisher. Any person who does any unauthorised act in relation to
this publication may be liable to criminal prosecution and civil claims for damages.

1 3 5 7 9 8 6 4 2

A CIP catalogue record for this book is available
from the British Library.

Printed and bound in China.

This book is sold subject to the conditions that it shall not, by way of trade or
otherwise, be lent, resold, hired out, or otherwise circulated without the publisher's
prior consent in any form or binding or cover other than that in which it is published
and without similar condition being imposed on the subsequent purchaser.

Author: Ian Graham
Illustrator: Annaliese Stoney
Editor: Nick Pierce

Visit
www.salariya.com
for our online catalogue and
free fun stuff.

SCIENCE STORIES

THE EUREKA MOMENT!™

MARIE CURIE
AND RADIOACTIVITY

WRITTEN BY
IAN GRAHAM

ILLUSTRATED BY
ANNALIESE STONEY

BOOK HOUSE
a SALARIYA imprint

INTRODUCTION

On November 7, 1867, a baby girl was born in Warsaw, Poland. She was to become one of the most famous and important scientists of the twentieth century. Her discoveries changed the world of science forever. They also led to new treatments for cancer and discoveries in atomic energy. In addition, she set up hundreds of new X-ray units in hospitals. Her name was Maria Sklodowska, but the world remembers her as Marie Curie.

She had to overcome many difficulties on her way to fame and success. She was born at a time when girls were not allowed to go to university in Poland, and women did not become research scientists. But she was very clever and full of ideas. She managed to find a way to go to university. Then she became the first woman in Europe to earn a doctorate in physics and the first woman to be a university professor in France. She taught and trained hundreds of other scientists. Many of them went on to make their own important discoveries.

The first book about her life was written by Eve, one of her two daughters. Eve could imagine that her mother would be puzzled by the idea of anyone wanting to read about her. She could imagine her mother saying, 'Eve, you're wasting your time. It's the science that matters, not the scientist.' Marie Curie was never interested in being famous. She turned away nearly all the reporters who tried to talk to her. But Eve would have told her mother, as she told friends, 'I am afraid that if I don't write this book, someone else will. Whoever it is, they cannot possibly know Marie Curie as well as I do. I fear they may get it wrong, so I must do it myself.'

As Eve prepared to start writing, she collected together all the letters, diaries and notes about her mother's life that she could find. She also went to Poland to talk to her mother's family. And of course she had a lifetime of her own memories. She remembered their visit to the United States when Marie Curie had become famous: the many prizes and awards she won, her pioneering medical work during the First World War and her historic scientific research. And she remembered the moments when her mother talked about her childhood and her work.

CHAPTER 1

1883

When I was 15 years old the grand master of education in Russian Poland, Monsieur Apushtin, visited my school. It was my last year there. We were all gathered together in the school hall. Then Monsieur Apushtin called out my name in a loud, deep voice - Maria Sklodowska. His voice echoed around the hall. When I walked out in front of everyone, he gave me a gold medal for graduating first in my year. My father expected nothing less, but he was very proud all the same.

MARIE CURIE'S FAMILY

The woman who would become Marie Curie was born in Warsaw on November 7, 1867, and named Maria Salomea Sklodowska. Her nickname in the family was Manya. Her father, Vladislav Sklodowski, was a professor who taught physics and mathematics. Her mother, Bronislawa, was the headmistress of a girls' school. Manya was the youngest of five children. When she was ten years old, her mother died from tuberculosis. Three years later her oldest sister, Sophie, died from a disease called typhus.

In Warsaw under Russian rule, girls couldn't
go any further in school or university. It wasn't
allowed. It was illegal to educate girls. Can you
believe it? Of course, we didn't put up with it. We
Poles are made of stronger stuff. We had to be. We
disobeyed the Russians who controlled our country
and their laws. Teachers carried on teaching Polish
girls, but they had to do it in secret. They gave
private lessons in people's homes and institutions
all over Warsaw. The classes moved around from
place to place to avoid discovery, so it was called
the Flying University. Anyone found breaking the
law could be sent to a freezing prison in Siberia, so
we had to be careful.

My older sister, Bronya, wanted to be a doctor.
The only way she could do it was to move
to Paris and study at the university there, the
Sorbonne. It was one of very few universities in
Europe that allowed women to study. But even

RUSSIAN POLAND

Poland was defeated several times in war during the nineteenth century. Its land was taken by its enemies and divided between them. Marie Curie grew up in part of Poland that belonged to the Russian Empire. The Russians banned the Polish language in schools, replaced Polish teachers with Russian ones, and burned Polish books. Polish children had to speak Russian at school. Poland would not be an independent country again until after World War I (1914-18).

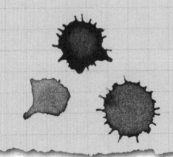

with her savings she didn't have enough money. Then I had an idea. I told Bronya, 'I have thought a lot about this problem. I've talked to father about it. And I think I have an answer.'

Bronya looked unsure. 'I can pay the train fare to Paris and have enough money to live on for one year. But the medical course is five years long. It's impossible.'

I explained my plan. 'If we struggle separately, we'll both fail, but if we work together...'

'What do you mean - work together?'

I said, 'Go to Paris and spend your money for as long as it lasts. Meanwhile, I will look for work as a governess. When your money runs out, father and I will be able to send you enough to carry on and finish your course. When you finish your studies, you can do the same for me. So with my plan, instead of failing we both succeed.'

And that's what we did. Bronya left for Paris and I worked as a governess. Father and I sent money to her and she finished her course. Just before she was to become a doctor, and she was about to marry another doctor, a letter arrived for me from Paris. I recognised the writing straight away. It was from Bronya telling me that it was finally my turn to come to Paris. But by then I had promised my old father that I would stay with him in Warsaw. After years working as a governess my dream of going to university in Paris had faded away. But Bronya persuaded me. She made me want to study again and, when my father agreed, I decided to go.

While I was waiting for my classes at the Sorbonne to begin, I went back to the wonderful

Flying University. And for the first time in my life I walked into a science laboratory. It was at the Museum of Industry and Agriculture. It was there that I did my very first science experiments. I felt so at home in the laboratory. I knew that this was what I was going to do for the rest of my life if I possibly could. I was ready to go to the Sorbonne.

And then it was time to leave for Paris. I bought the cheapest ticket - fourth class. The carriage, a ladies-only carriage, didn't even have any seats! I brought my own folding stool to sit on. It was a very long journey - more than a thousand miles by steam train. It took 40 hours. And the carriage was freezing cold. There was no heating in fourth class! I wrapped myself in a quilt to keep warm. I brought all the food and drink I'd need for the journey and read books to pass the time.

- Maria Sklodowska secretly attends school in Russian Poland, where it is illegal for girls to be educated.
- Maria works as a governess so that her sister can afford to study to become a doctor at the Sorbonne in Paris.
- Eventually, Maria gets her chance to begin university in Paris in 1891.

CHAPTER 2

1891

When I arrived in Paris, my sister Bronya's husband was waiting for me. He took me to their apartment, where I was to live until I could find my own place. A few days later, Bronya took me to the Sorbonne to sign up for classes. I signed the forms with the French version of my name, Marie. I was one of only 20 or so women amongst nearly 2,000 students at the

School of Sciences. I was amazed by how much freedom there was for students in Paris compared to schools in Poland. The students could choose whether or not to go to classes. They could even choose whether or not to sit exams at the end of their courses.

After all my years of hard work and scraping together money, I was finally studying science in wonderful, free, beautiful Paris. I couldn't have been happier. Every day I took a horse-drawn bus to the Sorbonne to hear great scientists giving lectures. I felt as if I had gone to heaven.

I was disappointed to find that my French was not quite as good as I thought it was. The professors who taught science often spoke too quickly for me to follow every word. I had to ask my fellow students what they'd said. I also thought I had been prepared well by my school, my

THE EIFFEL TOWER

When Marie Sklodowska arrived in Paris in 1891, a brand new structure towered over the city. A construction company led by Gustave Eiffel had designed and built it as the entrance to the 1889 World's Fair. We still know it today as the Eiffel Tower. It was the world's tallest man-made structure for 41 years. At first, hundreds of writers and artists protested against it. They thought it was an ugly iron blot on the face of a beautiful city. But soon it was hard to imagine Paris without the Eiffel Tower.

secret science lessons at the Flying University and everything my father had taught me. But I quickly discovered that I was not up to the standard needed for the Sorbonne. I had to work hard and put in long hours of extra study to catch up with the other students. I was constantly afraid that I would fail.

I scarcely remember anything of the next two years, because I studied so hard. Sometimes I even forgot to eat! Once, I was so hungry that I fainted. My big sister was horrified. She made me eat properly after that. The time flew by. It was the greatest time of my life. I took my final examination in July, 1893. A few days later I sat in the Sorbonne's great amphitheatre with 30 other students plus their friends and families to hear our results. I was trembling with fear. I held out my hands in front of me and saw that my fingers were actually shaking. My future, the rest of my life, depended on what the examiner was about to say. I couldn't bear the thought of going home to Poland as a failure and perhaps spending the rest of my life as a governess dreaming of the life I almost had... and then lost. I was jolted out of my daydream by the examiner's voice. When everyone had quietened down he said, 'I will read the results in the order of merit. The student with the highest score is... Marie Sklodowska!' I couldn't believe he'd just said my name. After fearing that I might have failed, I'd graduated with the highest score. I was the first woman ever to graduate top of the physics class. All my worries fell away and now I was trembling with excitement and relief instead of fear. I couldn't wait to get back to Poland and give my family the good news.

I knew what I should do next, but I didn't know how to do it. I'd learned how important mathematics is to science, so I wanted to go back to the Sorbonne and take a master's degree in maths. The problem was, I had no money left and my family couldn't support me any longer. They'd done more than enough to help me already. All seemed lost. I thought I'd probably look for work as a science teacher in Warsaw. Then a miracle happened. A scholarship fund that supported Polish students in other countries was told about me, and they decided to give me the money I needed. So, a few months later I was back in Paris, studying maths this time.

I graduated in maths in July 1894, but I felt a failure because I only managed to come second in my class. Soon after this I was asked to do some research into the magnetic properties of steel. It was important research for the new technology of electric motors and generators. I needed a laboratory to work in, but I couldn't find a good place. Then I was taken to meet someone who might be able to help me. I walked into a friend's apartment and saw a tall man standing by the French window. He had large eyes and brown hair. He seemed younger than his 35 years and he had the look of a dreamer. He was a professor of physics called Pierre Curie. He seemed very surprised to be meeting a physicist who was also

THE SORBONNE

The Sorbonne is one of the oldest parts of the University of Paris. King Louis IX's chaplain, Robert de Sorbon, created it in 1257 using a royal donation of money. It was the best-known part of the university and so the whole university became known as the Sorbonne.

a woman. It was a new experience for him. We got on with each other very well. When I went home to Poland in the Summer, he thought I had gone for good. He wrote to me again and again asking me to return to Paris. I remember one letter that said, 'It would be a fine thing to pass our lives near each other.' Eventually I gave in and went back to France. A year later we were married. Maria Sklodowska had become Marie Curie.

Just a few months later, we read about the discovery of X-rays by Wilhelm Roentgen. It caused quite a stir among scientists, because no-one knew that these rays existed or what they were. And then we heard that Henri Becquerel had discovered more rays coming from uranium. Roentgen had to use laboratory equipment and high-voltage electricity to produce his X-rays. But the uranium gave out rays without the need for any equipment or electricity to produce them.

They were entirely natural. I didn't know it at the time, but these two discoveries would shape the rest of my life.

- Maria has to work very hard to catch up to her fellow students in the School of Sciences at the Sorbonne.
- She graduates top of her class in physics in July 1893 and goes on to complete her study in mathematics in 1894.
- Maria meets and marries her fellow scientist, Pierre Curie, and becomes his wife, taking his surname.

30

X-RAYS

Wilhelm Roentgen (1845-1923) was a German scientist who was fascinated by devices called vacuum tubes. They were glass tubes that the air had been sucked out of. An electric current flowed through the tube between metal contacts called electrodes. In 1895, Roentgen found that these tubes could produce invisible rays that made a screen glow. He didn't know what they were so he called them X-rays. He discovered that they could pass through parts of the human body and make a shadow picture on photographic paper showing the bones inside the body.

WHO WAS
HENRI BECQUEREL?

Henri Becquerel (1852-1908) was
the French scientist who discovered
radioactivity. After Roentgen's discovery
of X-rays, Becquerel checked many
materials to see if they produced similar
rays. One day in 1896, he left a piece of
uranium in a drawer with a sheet of
photographic paper. When he developed
the paper (treated it with chemicals),
expecting to find nothing on it, he
actually found a dark mark. Invisible
rays from the uranium had darkened
the paper.

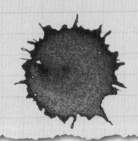

34

CHAPTER 3

1897

On a crisp, cold winter morning in 1897, I told my husband Pierre that I'd made an important decision. 'I want to try for a doctorate.'

He looked surprised.

I said, 'Isn't it the next step - degree, master's degree, doctorate?'

Pierre couldn't think of another woman in France with a science doctorate. 'If you're successful, you might be the first in France, maybe the first in the whole of Europe. I don't think it's ever been done before.' In fact, no woman anywhere in the world had yet been awarded a doctorate in science.

I said, 'Then it's high time that a woman did it, and it might as well be me.'

Pierre could see that I meant it. He sat quietly for a few moments, nodding slowly. Then he got up and walked over to our bookcase. He picked up an untidy stack of newspapers and science reports. I watched him, puzzled. 'What are you doing?'

'Well,' he said, 'if you're going to make history, you'll have to find the right subject for your research, won't you... unless you've chosen something already.'

I shook my head.

He put the papers on the dining table. 'Well, let's get started. There might be something here we can use.'

As we flicked through the science reports, Pierre suggested one idea. 'What about something to do with your work on steel?' He was talking about my research paper about the magnetic properties of steel.

'No. I want something completely new, totally different.'

'Why?'

ELEMENTS AND COMPOUNDS

Uranium is a type of substance called an element. Elements are made of particles of matter called atoms. There are lots of different types of atoms. An element is made of only one type of atom. When two or more atoms link together, they form a molecule. When different atoms or molecules link together, they form a substance called a compound. For example, water is a compound made of two elements, hydrogen and oxygen. Each water molecule is made of two hydrogen atoms linked to one oxygen atom.

It seemed obvious to me. 'I don't want to have to spend time reading through years of research to find out what's already been done. It'll take too long.'

Pierre said, 'You mean, you're too impatient!'

I wanted to find something that no-one had studied yet. Then I could start work on it in the laboratory straight away. The first possibility that came to me was Roentgen's X-rays. They had been found only a couple of years earlier, so they were a very recent discovery. At first thought, they seemed to be a promising choice. Then I realised that hundreds of scientific papers had already been written about them and more would be on the way.

Then we both said, 'Becquerel's uranium rays!' We looked through our science journals to check,

but there was little about these mysterious rays.
Although X-rays had attracted a lot of interest,
uranium rays seemed to have been ignored. Even
Becquerel hadn't carried out any further research.
As far as I could see, no-one in Europe was
studying them... yet. I made a decision. 'I have
found the subject for my research.'

I set to work in December 1897. Pierre persuaded
his boss to give me a room at the university to
work in. It was a small, damp workshop with a
dirt floor, but at least it was a space where I could
work. One day Pierre called in to see how I was
getting on and I had some news for him.

'Nothing seems to affect these uranium rays
- not light, not heat, not chemistry. I think
the rays must be coming from the uranium
atoms themselves.'

Pierre looked unsure. In fact, he was more than just unsure. He said, 'That's impossible.' At that time scientists thought atoms were the smallest possible building blocks of nature. They thought atoms couldn't be divided up into anything smaller or changed in any way. But if uranium rays were indeed coming from inside atoms, then scientists' ideas about atoms and what they were like must be wrong. Pierre said, 'If you're right, it changes everything. You'll need proof or no-one will believe you.'

He was right. It wasn't enough to have an idea or make a suggestion. I needed evidence to prove my theory. I said, 'If uranium atoms produce rays, maybe other atoms do it too. I'll have to test all sorts of materials, hundreds of them.' Pierre saw my shoulders fall. I must have looked quite sad.

He asked, 'Marie, what's wrong?'

'It's going to take so long,' I said. 'I'll have to leave each sample on top of a sheet of photographic paper overnight and then treat the paper with chemicals to see if it's been darkened by rays. And how do I measure the strength of the rays?' Then I remembered something about uranium that I could use to speed things up.

Air does not normally let electricity flow through it. Materials like this are called insulators. Henri Becquerel had already discovered that uranium, or its rays, changed the air around it so that electricity does flow through it. Materials that electricity can flow through are called conductors. Uranium changed air from an insulator to a conductor. I realised that I could use this.

I said to Pierre, 'Remember the instrument you invented with Jacques?' Jacques was his brother.

Pierre instantly knew what I was getting at. The instrument he had invented was an electrometer designed to measure the tiniest electric currents - currents so small that they couldn't be picked up at all on other instruments. Other scientists, including Becquerel, had tried to use it, but it was so difficult to operate that he couldn't manage it. I was sure I could use it to speed up the tests I'd have to do. I said, 'I can use it to test materials for radioactivity...'

Pierre stopped me. 'What is radioactivity?' He'd never heard the word before.

'Oh', I said, 'I can invent things too. I invented the word "radioactivity" to describe the rays given out by materials like uranium.' I went on, 'I can test a material for radioactivity very quickly. I use the instrument you invented to measure the size of an electric current passing through the air near it. If there's no electric current, it isn't radioactive. If there is a current, the material must be radioactive. The size of the current will show me how radioactive it is.'

Even with Pierre's help, it took me three weeks to learn how to use the electrometer and get reliable results.

My experiments went better than I ever imagined. I tested many different materials, but only samples containing uranium and another element, thorium, were radioactive. When I told Pierre, he couldn't have been happier for me. He clapped his hands and said, 'Fantastic!'

I had more to tell him. 'I tested some pitchblende today. I worked out how radioactive it should be, but when I tested it, the result was four times more than I expected. I couldn't quite believe it, so I repeated the test again and again. I got the same result every time.'

PITCHBLENDE

Pitchblende is a natural material that contains uranium and thorium. A piece of rock that is all made of the same mixture of substances, like pitchblende, is called a mineral. And minerals that contain valuable substances like uranium are called ores. Today, pitchblende is called Uraninite.

THE ELECTRIC CHARGE MAKES THE MIRROR SWIVEL ROUND, SO THE SPOT OF LIGHT MOVES ALONG THE RULER.

THEN I PUT THE SAMPLE I WANT TO TEST INSIDE THE TEST CHAMBER.

IF THE SAMPLE IS RADIOACTIVE, ITS RAYS CHANGE THE AIR ABOVE IT SO THAT A TINY ELECTRIC CURRENT CAN PASS THROUGH IT. THIS LETS THE ELECTRIC CHARGE DRAIN AWAY, MAKING THE LIGHT SPOT MOVE BACK ALONG THE RULER.

I TIME THE MOVEMENT. THE FASTER THE LIGHT MOVES, THE MORE RADIOACTIVE THE SAMPLE IS.

THAT'S REMARKABLE, MADAME.

47

Pierre looked through the measurements and calculations in my laboratory notebook. He didn't find any mistakes, but we couldn't make sense of the results. We talked to other scientists about it. They all thought that I must have made an error somewhere in my work. They looked down their noses at me and told me to do my experiments again and be more careful this time. But I knew I hadn't got it wrong. There had to be another reason for these unexpected results. When I thought more about it, the answer suddenly seemed obvious. The extra radiation must be coming from a new element, an element no-one had seen before. I was sure it was there and I had to find it. When I told Pierre, he agreed with me. He was so excited at the possibility of discovering a new element that he stopped his own research and came to work with me. We crushed some pitchblende to powder, heated it and mixed it with water, acids and other chemicals to divide it up into the different materials it contained. We finally produced a tiny sample, just a few grains of radioactive material. When I tested it, I wrote the result in my notebook. It was so surprising that I underlined it. I could scarcely believe it. Later, I read it out to Pierre, '150 times more active than uranium.' I'd done it. I'd found a new element.

Pierre said, 'You discovered it, so you can name it. What are you going to call it?'

I had already decided. 'My new element will be called polonium.' I named it after the country where I was born, Poland.

In December 1898, we returned to work after a short holiday. We thought there might be more to learn from pitchblende. We tested all the samples again and we found a second radioactive sample. We worked on it to purify it and found that whatever it contained was a million times more radioactive than uranium. A million! As soon as I saw the result I knew it couldn't be uranium, thorium or our new element, polonium. It must be another new element. I called it radium after its very strong radiation. Pierre and I decided to work mainly on radium from then on.

- Marie Curie decides to study for a doctorate. She chooses Henri Becquerel's newly-discovered uranium rays as her subject.
- She starts to think that the rays are coming from inside uranium atoms. She calls this phenomenon which she has discovered 'radioactivity'.
- She uses an electrometer to test which materials are radioactive. Whilst testing on pitchblende, she discovers two new highly-radioactive elements: polonium and radium.

CHAPTER 4

1899

Other scientists refused to believe that Pierre and I had discovered radium. They demanded more evidence. They wanted a sample of it that they could see and test and measure for themselves. At first, I thought it was impossible. There is such a tiny, tiny amount of radium in pitchblende that we would have to process tons of it to get just a pinch of radium for chemical tests.

Pitchblende is valuable because it contains uranium. We simply didn't have enough money to buy the huge amount of it that we needed.

Pierre refused to be beaten. He started an international search. He hoped that a friendly government or a generous mine somewhere might give us some pitchblende. A few of them did send small samples, but not nearly as much as we needed. Then Pierre found out about a uranium mine in Bohemia that was owned by the government. He asked a fellow scientist from the region what happened to all the waste rock from the mine after the uranium had been taken out. When he found out, he was so excited. He told me, 'They dump it in the forest! It's just sitting there and no-one wants it.'

'But, Pierre, we can't afford it.'

'Yes we can', he insisted. 'Pitchblende is so expensive because it contains uranium. But after the uranium has been taken out, the waste that's left behind is worthless. It still contains what we want though - radium. And it will save us months of work, because we won't have to take the uranium out. The mine has already done it for us. I've sent a message to the government asking if we can have a few tons of the waste. I told them it's for scientific research, not business. I told them that if our research is successful the waste could become valuable - the mine could sell it and make money out of it.'

When the answer came back, it wasn't exactly what we were hoping for. The government agreed to sell us a few tons of the waste at a low price, but it was still too expensive for us. All looked lost, but then suddenly everything changed. A geologist at the University of Vienna had heard about our problem. He persuaded the government to give us a ton of the waste free of charge if we would pay the transport costs. We couldn't afford even that. Luckily, a very wealthy man, Baron Edmond de Rothschild, heard about us. He agreed to pay the transport costs for us. And then he gave us enough money to buy several more tons of the pitchblende waste.

The next problem was where to do our work. Our little laboratory was far too small. We needed more space. The School of Physics and Chemistry at the university gave us a new 'laboratory', but when we went to see it we were shocked. An official took us to a courtyard in the university and said, 'Here is your new laboratory.'

I looked around. I couldn't see anything that looked like a laboratory. I was bewildered. I asked, 'Where, Monsieur?'

He pointed at a big old shed on one side of the courtyard. It was where medical students used to cut up dead bodies. It hadn't been used for such a long time that it was in a terrible state. Inside, there were a few dusty old tables, a blackboard and an ancient, rusty stove. The shed was freezing cold in winter and, because of glass skylights in the roof, it was boiling hot in summer. And the skylights were broken, so the roof leaked when it rained. It wasn't even good enough for dead bodies, but it was good enough for the Curies! We didn't have much time to feel sorry for ourselves, because the first truck-load of pitchblende arrived and we had to get to work.

I often spent the whole day stirring a huge cauldron of boiling, stinking pitchblende with a heavy iron rod almost as big as myself. We had to work outside in the open air, because our shed had no chimney to let the smoke and poisonous fumes escape. In the evening I often felt very tired. We were also using Pierre's brilliant electrometer to find out which of the materials we extracted from the pitchblende were radioactive. We thought this work might take a few months, but we spent four hard years doing this.

Most of the time we were alone, but sometimes we persuaded a technician or a student to come and help us. One of them, a young chemist called André Debierne, even discovered a third radioactive element in our pitchblende. He called it actinium.

The need to pay our bills was a constant problem. We just weren't earning enough money, so we both took on extra teaching work. It meant that we had less time to work on the pitchblende, so we just had to work harder. We were always exhausted.

As I purified the most radioactive part of the pitchblende, I kept wondering what the new element would look like. Pierre said, 'I should like it to have a beautiful colour.' Then one evening we went to our 'miserable old shed', as I called our laboratory. Before we lit the lamps I could see a bluish glow. Then another. And another. They were coming from tiny amounts of radium in glass bottles on the shelves and tables. The light from them was bright enough to read by. Pierre's wish had come true - radium did indeed have a beautiful colour.

Eventually, we managed to produce enough radium for tests that would prove whether or not it really is a new element. We gave the sample to Eugène Demarçay, an expert in a science called spectroscopy. He heated our sample until it glowed and looked at it through an instrument called a spectroscope. It spread out the light into a set of coloured lines called a spectrum. If Demarçay saw clear, sharp lines, then the sample must be a pure element. Each element produces its own spectrum, so if Demarçay saw a new pattern of coloured lines that had never been seen before, it was proof that we had a new element. Eight new elements had already been discovered in this way. I waited impatiently for his results, pacing up and down the laboratory. When he said the sample wasn't pure enough to get a clear spectrum, I was bitterly disappointed. Ten days later, I gave him a purer sample, but once again it wasn't good enough to produce a clear spectrum. I spent the next four months purifying a sample before I dared give it to Demarçay. This time it worked. He was able to see a clear, sharp spectrum and it was unlike any spectrum he'd ever seen before. We'd done it. Beyond any doubt, radium was an element, and it was a new element.

One of the things we discovered about radium is that it gives out heat. In fact, it produces enough heat to melt its own weight of ice and then boil the water. Heat is a form of energy, and all scientists know that energy cannot be created or destroyed. It can only change from one form to another. So the big question was - where does the energy that produces radium's rays and its light and heat come from? I thought it must be coming from inside the radium atoms, although I didn't know how. Pierre strongly disagreed with me. In the end, it was neither Pierre nor I who

ALPHA, BETA AND GAMMA

In 1899 the physicist Ernest Rutherford (1871-1937) found that two different types of rays come from radioactive elements. He called these two types of rays alpha and beta. Alpha rays are stopped by a sheet of paper. Beta rays go through paper, but they're stopped by a thin sheet of aluminium metal. In 1900, Paul Villard (1860-1934) discovered a third type of radiation, called gamma rays. They are so intense that a thick sheet of lead or many metres of concrete are needed to stop them. Alpha and beta rays are made of particles. Gamma rays are energy waves like light or radio, but far more intense.

solved this puzzle. It was a physicist from New Zealand called Ernest Rutherford.

We gave Rutherford another radioactive material called thorium X to study for his research. He found that it was less radioactive after a few days. It seemed to be disappearing, atom by atom. But the atoms themselves weren't vanishing. They were changing from thorium X atoms to different types of atoms. It's called transmutation. And each time they changed, they gave out a burst of energy. This was the energy that powered the mysterious rays. Pierre repeated Rutherford's experiments and finally agreed that Rutherford was right. And I had been right, too. The energy was coming from inside the atoms. It told scientists everywhere that their ideas about atoms being unchangeable were wrong. From then on, the race was on to find a way of looking inside atoms to find out what was going on

TO WIN OR NOT TO WIN!

Marie Curie nearly didn't win her Nobel Prize in 1903. When the Nobel Prize committee was thinking of awarding the prize to the Curies, four French scientists suggested giving the prize to Henri Becquerel and Pierre Curie, but not to Marie. They said she should not be mentioned! They couldn't believe that a woman could possibly have played an important part in such important research. When Pierre learned about this, he told the prize committee that they must include Marie or he would refuse to accept the award.

inside them. They had to be made of even smaller particles that carried energy in some way.

In June 1903, Pierre told me he'd been invited to give a talk about radium and radioactivity to the Royal Institution in London. He said yes straight away, because the Royal Institution is one of the most important science organisations. When we went into their meeting hall, it was crowded with famous scientists. They told me I was the first woman ever to be allowed to attend one of their meetings, but I wasn't allowed to give our talk. That was a step too far for them. Pierre had to speak for both of us. He described our research and carried out experiments in front of the audience. The lights were dimmed so that the scientists could see our radium glowing. They watched in silence as Pierre spoke. He couldn't speak English, so he spoke slowly in French and hoped they could follow what he was saying. I was so proud of him.

While we were in London, we were invited to grand dinners. I sat next to women wearing wonderful clothes and amazing jewellery. I amused myself by working out how many laboratories we could build with their sparkling diamonds.

Soon after we returned to Paris, we learned of an unbelievable announcement in Sweden. We had already won quite a few awards for our work, but not the most important scientific award of all - a Nobel Prize. It is given only for the greatest achievements. The announcement was that the Nobel Prize in Physics for that year, 1903, was to be given to Henri Becquerel, Pierre and I for our research and discoveries in radioactivity.

I had sent the final report of my research to examiners at the Sorbonne. It was called 'Researches on Radioactive Substances, by Madame Sklodowska Curie'. On June 12, 1903, it was time for me to answer their questions about it so that they could decide whether or not to give me a doctorate. My sister Bronya had persuaded me to buy a new dress for the occasion. The room was full of other scientists and students. They sat in silence as three examiners asked me questions about my research. The examiners listened carefully to my answers. I soon knew their decision. At the end of the meeting, they had a short discussion and then one of them announced, 'The University of Paris accords you the title of doctor of physical science.' The audience started clapping. I had finally achieved what I'd set out to do six years earlier. What a lot Pierre and I had packed into those six years.

Soon afterwards, Pierre and I had to make an important decision. American companies wanted to use our methods to produce radium and other substances from pitchblende that they could sell and make profits from. They couldn't do it without our help and permission. We could choose to charge them for the right to use our methods and it would make us a fortune. However, we quickly decided to give away all of our work and secrets to the world free of charge. We thought it was the right thing to do.

Eight years later, in 1911, Marie Curie learned that she had been awarded the Nobel Prize in chemistry. This made her the first person ever to be awarded two Nobel Prizes and she is still the only person ever to have won two Nobel Prizes in two different sciences - an extraordinary achievement.

RADIUM

Today, we know that radium is a silvery-white metal. When it makes contact with air, a chemical reaction turns the surface of radium black. It glows with a pale blue light. When it is heated, it melts at a temperature of 700°C (1,292°F) and boils at 1,737°C (3,159°F). It is very dangerous because of the radiation it gives out and because of a radioactive gas called radon that it produces.

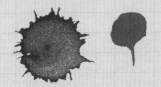

- Marie and Pierre are given a new laboratory in the School of Physics and Chemistry at the Sorbonne where they can carry out research.
- Marie and Pierre's research contributes, with the work of physicist Ernest Rutherford, to changing the scientific understanding of atoms. It is now understood that atoms can change and that the energy released in this process, called transmutation, is what gives off the radioactive rays in elements like radium.
- Marie and Pierre Curie and Henri Becquerel win the 1903 Nobel Prize in Physics for their work. Marie is awarded the title of doctor of physical science after completing her doctorate.

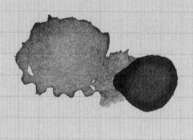

CHAPTER 5

1914

A s 1914 began, I was bringing up my two beautiful daughters, Irène and Eve, on my own. My husband, Pierre, had died in a road accident eight years earlier. Life went on, but I was very unhappy. He was in my thoughts all the time and I missed him dreadfully.

The Sorbonne asked me to take Pierre's place. I became the first woman professor there and

THE DEATH OF PIERRE CURIE

On the afternoon of April 19, 1906, it was raining heavily in Paris. Pierre Curie rushed along, using an umbrella to keep himself dry. As he crossed a busy street, the Rue Dauphine, he stepped out from behind a cab and slipped under the hooves of two horses pulling a heavy wagon. Somehow, the stamping hooves all missed him. He also passed safely between the wagon's front wheels. Just when it seemed that he might survive without a scratch, one of the wagon's rear wheels rolled over his head and he died instantly.

head of research in the science department. I taught Pierre's science classes and also carried on with my own research. I no longer had to work in my 'miserable shed' of a laboratory. I'd fought hard to have a new laboratory built, but the university kept delaying. When it looked like they were going to back out of their promise to build it, I threatened to leave. That did the trick. The university finally built a new laboratory for scientific research into radioactive materials, which I headed. The Pasteur Institute built a laboratory next to it for medical research. The two laboratories together were known as the Radium Institute.

Towards the end of July 1914, my new office was ready for me to move into, and the laboratory equipment had started arriving. I was soon working hard in the laboratory and my office. Everyone was busy and looking forward to this

new adventure for all of us. The whole site was
a hive of activity. Two days later, it was empty.
Almost everyone had left. War had broken
out in Europe. German troops were invading
France, and all my staff had gone to fight in
the war. I wondered how many of our friends
and colleagues would return and how many we
might never see again. I couldn't believe that after
thousands of years of science and education, we
were still settling our differences by killing each
other. It's horrible.

I soon learned that hospitals in Paris were
short of X-ray equipment to help treat wounded
soldiers. I gathered up all the unused equipment I
could find in universities and doctors' offices, and
took it to the hospitals.

At the beginning of September, a government
official arrived at the Institute. He instructed me

WHAT ARE X-RAYS?

X-rays are made of electric and magnetic energy waves travelling together. It's called electromagnetic radiation. Other forms of electromagnetic radiation include light and radio waves. X-rays have much shorter waves. They can pass through the soft parts of a human body, but they are blocked by hard bones, so doctors use X-rays to look inside the human body without having to cut it open.

to take all the radium I had to Bordeaux to stop it from falling into enemy hands. The government had already left Paris and moved south to Bordeaux to escape from the advancing troops. My whole stock of radium amounted to just one gram, not even a teaspoonful, but after it was packed inside a heavy lead box, I could barely lift it. It was probably worth a million francs, but I decided to take it to Bordeaux myself, alone.

The train from Paris was crowded with people fleeing from the capital. One said he had heard guns firing to the north of the city. Another said she had seen flashes in the night from the big guns. When we got to Bordeaux, a fellow passenger took pity on me and helped me to take my heavy bag to a hotel. He had no idea he was holding a million francs! The next day, I handed my radium over to Professor Bergonie at the University of Bordeaux Faculty of Sciences. I returned to Paris on a packed military train. A kind soldier sitting next to me shared his sandwiches with me.

On my return to Paris, I was keen to do my bit for the war effort in whatever way I could. When

the government asked citizens to give up their gold
and silver to help pay for the war, I looked at all
the medals and prizes I had been awarded for my
work. They were just ornaments gathering dust,
so I offered them to the government to be melted
down. My offer was declined, but I soon found
another way to help.

I had supplied hospitals in Paris with X-ray
equipment. Then I learned that hospitals closer to
the fighting, where many of the wounded soldiers
were being treated, had no X-ray equipment. The
whole French Army had only one X-ray unit of
its own. Because of this, badly wounded soldiers
required long, serious operations to find bullets and
pieces of shrapnel so that surgeons could remove
them. Lives were being lost. I knew that X-rays
would show every piece of metal and broken bone
in a soldier's body. Sadly, many of the soldiers
were too badly wounded to survive the journey to

X-ray units in Paris. It seemed obvious to me that the X-ray equipment should go to the soldiers, not the other way round. I knew what I had to do.

First, I took a course in how to use an X-ray machine for medical imaging instead of scientific research. Then I raised enough money to have a car turned into an X-ray unit. The X-ray equipment was carried in the back of the car. It was powered by a generator driven by the car's engine.

When rich people heard what I was doing, they started giving more cars and money. In no time, I had 20 'radiological cars'. I worked in one of them myself, with my daughter Irène as my assistant. Soon we were heading north to the battlefields. Delays and breakdowns made me angry, because lives depended on us. We had a driver, but I learned to drive so that I could take over if the

WORLD WAR I

World War I started in July 1914 and ended just over four years later on November 11, 1918. It was triggered in part by the assassination of the Archduke Franz Ferdinand of Austria during a visit to Sarajevo, Serbia. This set off a series of events that led to war breaking out between Germany and France, which drew in Britain and other countries in Europe plus Russia, Japan and the United States of America. By the end of the war, about 16 million soldiers, sailors, air crew and civilians had been killed.

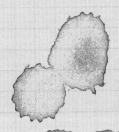

driver wasn't available. I also took a course in car mechanics so that I could repair the engine or change a wheel if we broke down.

To begin with, many of the soldiers were quite terrified of my X-ray equipment, but they quickly realised how important it was to their treatment. They nicknamed my radiological cars the 'Little Curies'. We usually worked in local hospitals. I set up an X-ray room in each hospital and trained the staff to use it. By the end of the war my radiological unit had set up 220 X-ray rooms at hospitals in addition to our 20 'Little Curies'. Together, they examined more than a million wounded soldiers during the war.

When Paris was no longer at risk of invasion, I brought my precious radium back there and continued my work. I studied radium's chemistry, the compounds it makes and its radioactivity. On November 11, 1918, we heard the most wonderful news. The war was finally over. I rushed out to buy a French flag to fly from the Radium Institute, but the shops had already sold them all. There wasn't a single French flag to be had anywhere. I had some flags made by stitching red, white and blue material together and then I flew them from the institute's windows.

Newspaper reporters kept bothering me. They wanted to meet me and write articles about me, but I had no time for them. It was the science that was important, not me. And the science was published in science journals, so I saw no reason to give interviews. What was the point? But one of the reporters refused to take no for an answer. She kept talking to all sorts of people until she found someone who would introduce her to me.

89

I gave in and agreed to talk to her for a few minutes. She was an American journalist called Marie Mattingly Meloney. She proved to be an extraordinary woman.

I told Mrs Meloney how unhappy I was at how little radium I had - just one gram, not even a thimbleful. I told her, 'The United States has 50 times as much radium as I have. Even the city of New York has seven times more radium than the whole of France.'

She was shocked. She thought I must be earning a fortune from radium production and so I would have as much radium as I could produce or buy, but I told her there was no money. Pierre and I had given away our secrets for nothing. After just a moment's thought, she said, 'Madame Curie, I will raise the money you need to buy more radium.' Against my better judgement, I even

MARIE MATTINGLY MELONEY

The New York Times newspaper described Marie Meloney (1878-1943) as one of the leading women journalists of the United States. Nicknamed Missy, her mother and her husband were newspaper editors and she herself worked as a journalist from the age of 15. When she met Marie Curie in 1920, she was the editor of a fashion and arts magazine called *The Delineator*, published in New York.

agreed to go to the United States with her if her fundraising was successful. I thought no more about it, relieved to have got through my first press interview. I didn't think I'd hear from her again.

When I got back to the laboratory after a short break, I was amazed to find a large pile of letters waiting for me. Most of them were from America. When I opened them, they were from people looking forward to seeing me in the United States. They were asking me to give lectures, let them use my name to sell their products, appear at all sorts of events and send autographs and photographs of myself. Someone even wanted my permission to name his race-horse after me! Mrs Meloney's fund-raising campaign had been very successful indeed, so it looked like I was going to have to visit the United States after all.

I thought I'd be going for two weeks at most, but Mrs Meloney persuaded me to stretch it to two months. When I told her how much I would miss my daughters, she urged me to bring them with me. Then she stunned me when she said she'd arranged for the US President to present me with a gram of radium. I was very impressed!

On May 4, 1921, I boarded the ocean liner *Olympic* at Cherbourg. My room was so grand that I felt like a movie star. I survived the voyage quite well. I felt a little light-headed at times, but I didn't suffer from sea-sickness.

When we arrived in New York, I started to feel quite worried, because Mrs Meloney had arranged for me to speak with the press. I sat in an armchair on the boat deck while a group of rather excitable reporters, photographers and men with film cameras crowded around me. They shouted questions at me and told me to look this way and that for their photographs. It was quite a mad affair, like nothing I'd experienced before.

CROSSING THE OCEAN

When Marie Curie visited the United States, the only way she could cross the Atlantic Ocean was by ship. Two British airmen, John Alcock (1892-1919) and Arthur Whitten Brown (1886-1948) had made the first non-stop flight across the ocean only two years earlier. The American pilot Charles Lindbergh (1902-1974) made the first solo transatlantic flight in 1927. Regular passenger flights across the Atlantic began in 1928, using giant airships. Crossings by passenger aeroplanes did not begin until the 1930s.

By the time I was able to leave the ship, there were thousands of people on the dockside waving flags at me and handing me bunches of flowers. There were even brass bands playing the Polish and French national anthems. A millionaire, Andrew Carnegie, had sent a limousine to collect me and take me to Mrs Meloney's home. I was beginning to realise how important my discovery of radium had become.

The evening newspapers had reports of my arrival. One of them made me so angry. It claimed that I'd come to the United States to 'end all cancer.' I showed the headline to Mrs Meloney and told her, 'I didn't say that. It's wrong, wrong, wrong!'

She promised me that she would phone the paper and have it corrected. Then she said that several universities and colleges wanted to give me honorary degrees, so I'd have to wear my academic cap and gown. I must have looked a little surprised or puzzled, because she said, 'You have brought them with you, haven't you?'

I had not, because I had never owned an academic cap and gown. Mrs Meloney was horrified. She called in a tailor who delivered a brand new black silk gown. I hated it. The 'mortarboard' cap that came with it made me look ridiculous. In the end, after much discussion, I reluctantly agreed to wear the gown, but definitely not the cap!

I had to go to endless dinners and speeches. At one of them, I told the audience something I felt very strongly about. I said, 'When radium was discovered, no-one knew that it would prove useful in hospitals. The work was one of pure science. And this is proof that scientific work must be done for its own sake and the beauty of science. Then there is always the chance that it may become, like radium, a benefit for humanity.'

Then the great day arrived. On May 20, President Harding welcomed me to the White House in Washington DC. He presented me with a gram of radium. Well, that's what everyone thought, but actually he presented me with an empty box. The radium was so valuable and so dangerous because of its radioactivity that there was none of it in the box. It was held elsewhere in a safe, secure place.

I was exhausted by the end of the tour. On June 28, I left for France on the *Olympic* with my precious radium locked in the ship's safe.

It was worth $100,000. Mrs Meloney had raised enough money to buy even more radioactive chemicals worth tens of thousands of dollars. And more money was still arriving.

- Marie Curie becomes the first female professor at the Sorbonne after the sudden death of her husband in 1906.
- She leads a campaign to have cars carrying x-ray units sent to soldiers serving on the frontline in World War One so that they can receive better medical treatment. Marie and her daughter drive one of the vehicles and help in hospitals.
- The American journalist Marie Mattingly Meloney takes Marie Curie on a fundraising tour of the United States to raise money to buy radium for further research. Marie meets the President of the United States, Warren G Harding, and raises many thousands of dollars.

98

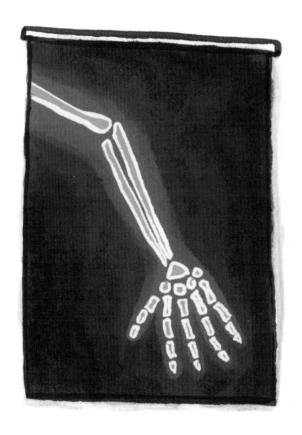

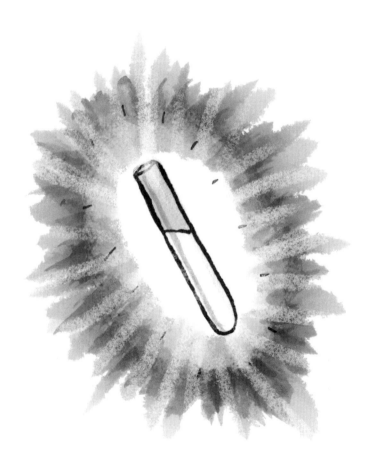

CHAPTER 6

1925

The French Academy of Medicine asked me to help them draw up safety measures for working with radium. I always believed that the way we handled it in the laboratories was safe. Other people were harmed by it because they weren't scientists and didn't understand it. Greedy fake doctors were selling all sorts of made-up tonics and so-called medicines containing radium.

Someone calling himself Alfred Curie sold a radium skin cream called Crème Tho-Radia. There was radium toothpaste, radium boot polish and radium drinks. Radium plant food claimed to grow bigger, healthier plants. Of course, it was all nonsense.

People mistakenly thought radium was safe because it was natural. Why? How stupid is that? Plants contain all sorts of poisons that are natural. It doesn't mean that they're safe. Deadly nightshade and snake venom are natural. Are they safe? Of course not. But people painted radium on their teeth and lips to make them glow at parties! Dancers painted it on their bodies and costumes to make them glow on stage. What were they thinking?

Everyone should have known that radium could be dangerous. Wasn't it used to treat cancer?

HOW DANGEROUS IS RADIUM?

Both Marie and Pierre Curie suffered from burns, aching joints, tiredness and anaemia caused by radiation from radium. Some of Marie's own former students were among 140 scientists who had died by 1925 after working with radium. Workers in industries that used radium suffered harm from it too. And many of the people who regularly drank radium tonics for their health died from radiation poisoning. Radium was, and is, highly dangerous because of its radioactivity.

WHAT IS CANCER?

A healthy human body is made of trillions of living cells. There is a constant need for new cells for growth and to replace cells that have died. Healthy cells divide in two to make the new cells needed. If this goes wrong, cells may divide again and again, making far more cells than the body needs. The extra cells, which may not work properly, can spread and carry on dividing. The bad cells can damage vital organs. This is cancer.

THE RADIUM GIRLS

In the 1920s, women working with clocks and watches in the USA and Canada started falling ill. Some of them died. Their job was to apply radium paint to the hands and numbers on the faces of clocks and watches so that they glowed in the dark. The women brought their paintbrush to a fine point by stroking it between their lips. It caused a serious illness that became known as radium jaw and the women were known as the radium girls.

And how did it do that? It worked by killing cancer cells. Tubes of radium placed on the skin killed the cells.

I remember when we started working with pitchblende, we gave a little glass tube of chemicals from it containing radium to Henri Becquerel. He put it in his pocket and when he took it out several hours later he noticed a small burn on his skin under the tube. I had also suffered burns while carrying radium.

Pierre even studied the effects of radium on living flesh by deliberately putting some radium on his arm to see what would happen. He was quite delighted when a burn appeared. He measured it and noted that it covered an area of six square centimetres. It grew redder and redder over the next few days. On the twentieth day,

he came to me with a wide grin on his face and showed me his arm. 'Look, Marie', he said, 'a scab has formed over my burn.'

The wound became so serious that it had to be bandaged. On the 42nd day, new skin started forming around the edges. Even after 52 days, the wound had not yet completely healed. It left a grey mark on his skin, which showed that the damage ran quite deep. So, you see, we knew that radium could cause physical changes from our earliest days working with it. We understood that it had to be handled carefully.

When the Academy of Medicine produced its report, they advised scientists to work behind metal screens, handle radium with tongs and store it in thick metal containers. The Academy also said that that scientists should have regular blood tests to check on their health. We already

WHERE DOES ATOMIC ENERGY COME FROM?

It takes so much energy to smash particles of matter together with enough force to make atoms that this process normally only happens inside stars. If the particles at the centre of an atom, called the nucleus, come apart again this enormous energy is released. This is the energy that makes radium glow and give out heat. It is also the energy used by nuclear power stations to produce electricity, and released suddenly when atomic bombs explode.

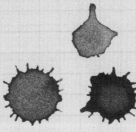

knew all of that. Many of my fellow scientists already did these things to stay safe. I didn't bother with them myself. I never felt that radium was a danger to me.

My dear Pierre had warned about another danger that worried him. He spoke about it in his Nobel Prize lecture in 1903. He said, 'In criminal hands radium could be dangerous.' My son-in-law, Frédéric - my daughter Irène's husband - spoke about an even more worrying use of radium and other radioactive substances. He said that if scientists ever discover how to release the energy locked up inside atoms, it could be used for good or bad. It could make a devastating weapon, a bomb of immense power. Our calculations showed that just one pound of radium, which you could hold in one hand, contained as much energy as a large power station could produce in a whole year.

And if a way could be found to release all of this energy at once, it would be more powerful than any bomb then known. Just one of these 'atomic bombs' could create a massive fireball and wipe out a whole city. Imagine that. It would be like hell on Earth.

Marie Curie hoped that scientists would never discover how to use atomic energy in war. In fact, they did discover how to release massive amounts of energy from atoms and use it as a terrifying weapon, but she didn't live to see it. Eleven years after her death, World War II was ended by the use of the first atomic bombs. One was dropped by the United States on the Japanese city of Hiroshima, destroying the city and killing thousands of its people. A second bomb destroyed another Japanese city, Nagasaki. Japan surrendered, bringing the war to an end.

- A radium craze sweeps around the world in the 1920s. Fake doctors sell harmful or useless products to the public who don't understand the dangers of radioactive materials.
- During World War Two, other scientists carry out further research into radium in order to develop very powerful atomic bombs. The world becomes a more dangerous place.

EPILOGUE

In June, 1934, the 66-year-old Marie Curie travelled to the Sancellemoz sanatorium in Passy, southeast France. She checked in under the name Madame Pierre so newspaper reporters wouldn't recognise her. Her daughter, Eve, was with her. A well-known doctor, Professor Roch, had come from Geneva, Switzerland, to see her. As a nurse showed him to her room, he asked, 'How is Madame Curie this morning?'

The nurse looked serious. 'She seems a little better today, although she's still very weak.' Her temperature had reached 40°C (104°F) the previous day.

When they arrived at her room, they found Marie sitting up in her bed with Eve at her bedside. Marie asked Roch, 'Professor, do you have any news for me?'

'I have indeed, Madame.' He held up a handful of X-rays. 'As you know, your X-rays showed no sign of lung problems.' Her doctors had thought she might be suffering from tuberculosis, the illness that had claimed her mother's life. However, X-rays of her chest revealed no signs of it in her lungs. Her illness remained a mystery until doctors carried out a series of blood tests.

The professor continued, 'The answer was in your blood. Madame, you are suffering from pernicious anaemia. I can assure you that you do not have tuberculosis and also that you will not need surgery.'

Anaemia is an illness caused by a shortage of healthy red blood cells. Pernicious anaemia is a very serious form of the illness. Surprisingly, Marie was visibly relieved by the professor's news. She had been worrying that she may be suffering from a condition that would need an operation. It worried her because her father had died after an operation.

While the professor held up one of her X-rays to the window for another look, Marie's daughter said, 'Professor, did you know it was my mother who enabled more doctors to use X-rays during the war?'

'So, Madame Curie,' said Roch, 'without your work during the war, I might not be looking at your X-rays today.'

'Perhaps'

Her daughter Eve added, 'Everything that has happened came from one Eureka Moment, when you thought that uranium's rays might be coming from inside its atoms. No-one believed Marie Curie when she said that, but she proved them all wrong. Thanks to that, humanity has discovered polonium and radium, new ideas about atoms and atomic energy, and developed new cures for cancer. '

The doctor went on, 'Your work on radium may have made history, Madame Curie, but it's also probably why you're here now and feeling so ill.'

Marie disagreed. She insisted that her illness was nothing to do with radium and that all she needed to do was to fill her lungs with the pure, clean mountain air and she would be sure to recover. Nurses had been taking her temperature every hour and she made sure that they gave her the results. She said, 'But, doctor, my temperature is coming down. My fever is going. That's a good sign, isn't it?'

The professor smiled at her, but said nothing.

She was more seriously ill than she knew. In fact, she was dying, but her daughter, Eve, insisted that she should not be told. Her falling temperature was not a sign that she was fighting off her fever. It was a sign that her body was failing. Later that day she slipped into a coma. Eve and one of her doctors, Pierre Lowys, took turns to sit with her overnight. At sunrise the next morning, July 4, 1934, Marie Curie's heart stopped beating. Her death made front-page news all over the world.

Two days later, she was given a small funeral with only family, friends and co-workers there. She was buried alongside her husband, Pierre, near their home in Sceaux in the south of Paris. Scientists and historians were keen to read her laboratory notes and learn from them. Sadly, her notebooks were found to be too radioactive for anyone to handle safely without wearing protective clothing.

Eve Curie's book about her mother was published in France, Britain, the United States and several other countries at the same time in 1937. It was an award-winning best-seller.

In 1995, Marie's remains and those of her husband, Pierre, were moved. Before Marie's body was taken out of the ground, it was tested for radioactivity. The illness that took her life was thought to be due to years of radiation damage caused by working with radium. This could have made her body dangerously radioactive, but scientists were surprised to find very low levels of radioactivity. It was a puzzle. Her illness had been caused by radiation, but it didn't appear to be radiation from radium. A high dose of X-rays could have caused the same illness without making her body radioactive. Because of this, scientists now think it may have been her work with X-rays during World War I that led to her death. She'd taken thousands of X-ray images with equipment that was not properly shielded. She could easily have received a deadly dose of the rays.

Her remains were moved to a building called the Panthéon in Paris, where the most famous French citizens are buried. Marie Curie was the first woman to receive this great honour for what she had done during her life. Thousands of people, including the French president, attended the event to show their respect for Marie and Pierre Curie. The little girl from Poland had come a very long way indeed. In addition to her very important work on radioactivity, she had also made it easier for all the women who came after her to study at university, become scientists and be recognised for their work.

126

TIME LINE

1867

Maria Salomea Sklodowska (known as Manya) is born in Warsaw on November 6.

1883

Manya graduates from school and is awarded a gold medal.

1886

Manya begins work as a governess.

1891

Manya, now known as Marie, arrives in Paris to begin studying physics at the Sorbonne (University of Paris).

1893

Marie graduates in physics, top of her class.

1894

Marie receives a master's degree in mathematics and meets Pierre Curie.

1895

Marie and Pierre Curie are married.
Wilhelm Roentgen discovers X-rays.
The Lumière brothers show the first films
in Paris.

1897

Marie and Pierre Curie's first child, a
daughter called Irène, is born.
Marie begins work on her doctorate.

1898

Marie and Pierre discover a new element,
which Marie names polonium after her
home country, Poland.
Later, she discovers a second new element,
radium.

1901

Queen Victoria dies.

1903

Marie is awarded a doctorate in science and becomes the first woman to be awarded a Nobel Prize (in physics), which she shares with Pierre and Henri Becquerel.
The Wright brothers build and fly the first powered aircraft.
A major earthquake destroys San Francisco, USA.

1904

Pierre Curie begins teaching at the Sorbonne. Pierre and Marie's second child, another daughter called Eve, is born.

1905

The German-born physicist Albert Einstein publishes a series of scientific papers. One of them explains his theory of relativity. It is one of the most important scientific theories of the twentieth century.

1906

Pierre Curie dies in a road accident in Paris. Marie takes his place at work and becomes the Sorbonne's first female professor.

1908

Ford begins production of its Model T car.

1911

Marie wins a second Nobel Prize, in chemistry this time. She is the first woman to win a second Noble Prize and also the only person ever to win Nobel Prizes in two different sciences.

Ernest Rutherford discovers the structure of the atom.

1912

The ocean liner RMS Titanic sinks during its maiden voyage from Britain to New York, with the loss of more than 1,500 lives.

1914

World War I begins.

Marie takes her radium to Bordeaux for safe-keeping during the war, so that it does not fall into enemy hands. She also creates a fleet of 20 mobile X-ray units, which are used to help treat wounded soldiers.

1917
The United States enters World War I.
The Russian emperor and his family are
executed after a revolution. The Soviet
Union is created in Russia.

1918
World War I ends with the defeat of
Germany.
The Radium Institute opens in Paris.

1919
Two British airmen, Alcock and Brown,
make the first non-stop flight across the
Atlantic Ocean.

1921

Marie makes the first of two trips to the USA.

1925

Scottish inventor John Logie Baird transmits the first television pictures.

1927

American airman Charles Lindbergh makes the first solo non-stop flight across the Atlantic Ocean.

American inventor Philo Farnsworth makes the first all-electronic television system.

The Jazz Singer, the first 'talkie' (a film with sound) is made.

1928

Alexander Fleming discovers penicillin, the first modern antibiotic (bacteria-killing) medicine.

1929

A serious economic crisis called The Great
Depression begins in the USA and lasts until
World War II.
Marie Curie makes her second visit to the
USA.

1932

A second Radium Institute opens in Poland,
run by Marie's sister, Bronya.

1934

Marie Curie dies on July 4 from anaemia,
probably caused by years of exposure to
radiation from radium and X-rays during
World War I.

1995

The remains of Marie and Pierre Curie are
moved to the Panthéon in Paris, where
France's greatest citizens are buried.

GLOSSARY

academic gown A loose-fitting, long-sleeved garment, usually black, worn by those who have been awarded a university degree.

alpha radiation Particles given out by some radioactive materials. Each alpha particle is made of four smaller particles.

anaemia An illness caused by a shortage of healthy red blood cells or a shortage of a substance called haemoglobin that is found in red blood cells. Someone who suffers from anaemia may feel tired, weak and short of breath.

aplastic anaemia An illness caused by the body's inability to make blood cells because of damaged bone marrow.

assassination The killing of someone for political reasons.

atom The smallest part of an element.

beta radiation Particles given out by some radioactive materials.

cancer A disease caused by uncontrolled division of cells in part of the body.

coma A period of unconsciousness from which someone cannot be woken.

compound A substance made of two or more different types of atoms linked together.

conductor A substance that lets heat, sound or electricity pass through it easily.

doctorate The highest level of academic degree awarded by a university.

electric current A river-like flow of electrically charged particles moving in the same direction.

electromagnetic radiation Rays made of electric and magnetic waves travelling through space together. Light, radio waves, X-rays and gamma rays are electromagnetic.

element One of more than 100 materials that cannot be broken down into simpler substances. Elements are made of atoms. Each element is made of its own type of atom. For example, hydrogen is an element and it is made of hydrogen atoms.

energy The ability to do work. There are lots of different forms of energy, including heat, electrical, mechanical and magnetic energy.

franc The unit of money used in France and several other European countries until it was replaced by the euro in 2002.

gamma radiation One of the three types of radiation given out by radioactive elements. Gamma radiation is made of rays like light, radio waves and X-rays, but gamma rays have shorter waves and carry more energy.

geologist A scientist who studies the Earth and the natural processes that have shaped it since its formation.

governess A woman who teaches an employer's children at their home.

graduate Somebody who has completed a course of study at a university.

honorary degree An academic degree awarded to someone because of his or her important work, not because he or she has completed a course of study.

insulator A substance that does not let heat, sound or electricity pass through it easily.

laboratory A room or building where scientists learn or carry out research.

limousine A big, luxurious car, often driven by a professional driver called a chauffeur.

liner A large, luxurious passenger ship that carries people on regular long-distance voyages according to a timetable.

master's degree An academic degree awarded to someone who has completed a course of study at a higher level than a bachelor's degree.

monsieur A French word used to address a man in the same way as 'mister' or 'sir' in English.

mortarboard An academic cap with a square, flat top, named after the flat board used by bricklayers to hold mortar.

Nobel Prizes International prizes awarded for outstanding achievements in physics, chemistry, physiology or medicine, literature, economics and work helping to bring about peace. The prizes are named after the Swedish scientist Alfred Nobel (1833-1896), who invented dynamite and left money after his death to fund the prizes.

nucleus The particle or particles at the centre of an atom. The nucleus has a positive electric charge, which is balanced by the negative electrical charge of electrons travelling around the nucleus.

particle A tiny amount of matter.

pernicious anaemia An illness, a type of anaemia, caused by a shortage of healthy red blood cells.

professor The highest level of university teacher or lecturer.

radiation Particles or electromagnetic waves given out by a substance.

radioactivity The production of particles or electromagnetic waves by the nuclei of radioactive elements.

ray a stream of particles or waves travelling through space.

scholarship A sum of money paid to help a student complete a course of study.

shrapnel Pieces of metal thrown out by bombs following an explosion.

Sorbonne One of the oldest parts of the University of Paris, set up in the 13th century.

spectroscopy The scientific study of light given out by, or affected by, matter.

spectrum The colours that light contains, spread out so that all the individual colours can be seen.

surgeon A doctor trained to carry out surgery (treatment by cutting into the body and repairing or removing diseased or injured parts).

transmutation The changing of one element into another by the process of radioactivity (giving out particles or waves).

tuberculosis An infectious disease that usually affects the lungs.

typhus An infectious disease spread by fleas and lice that causes fever, headache and a rash on the skin.

uranium A chemical element that gives off radioactive rays. It has been used as a fuel in nuclear power stations and in the first nuclear bombs.

x-rays Very short electromagnetic waves that can pass through materials that light cannot pass through. X-rays are used in hospitals to make pictures that show bones and other structures inside the human body.

INDEX